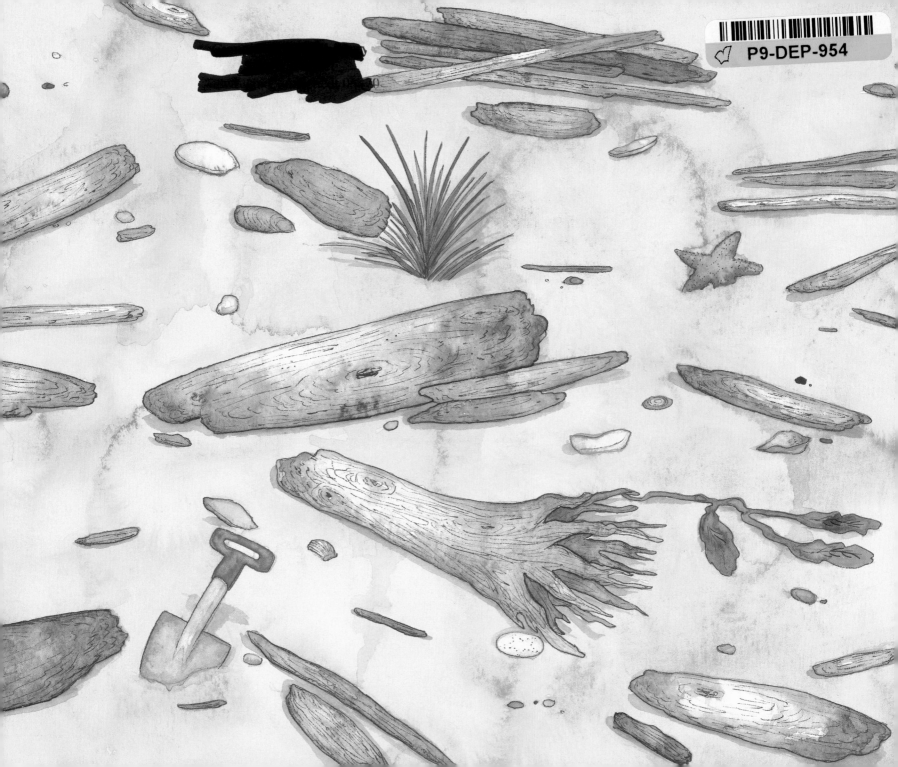

BOATS FOR PAPA

JESSIXA BAGLEY

A NEAL PORTER BOOK

ROARING BROOK PRESS

NEW YORK

A Neal Porter Book

Published by Roaring Brook Press

Roaring Brook Press is a division of Holtzbrinck Publishing Holdings Limited Partnership

175 Fifth Avenue, New York, New York 10010

The art for this book was created with pen and watercolor on paper.

mackids.com

Library of Congress Cataloging-in-Publication Data

Bagley, Jessixa, author.

Boats for Papa / Jessixa Bagley. — First edition.

pages cm

"A Neal Porter Book."

Summary: Buckley and his mother cope with the loss of their
father/husband by sending small wooden boats, built by Buckley, off into
the ocean.

ISBN 978-1-62672-039-8 (hardcover) — ISBN 1-62672-039-8 (hardcover)

1. Grief—Juvenile fiction. 2. Mother and child—Juvenile fiction. 3.
Boats and boating—Juvenile fiction. [1. Grief—Fiction. 2. Mother and
child—Fiction. 3. Boats and boating—Fiction. 4. Handicraft—Fiction.]
I. Title.

PZ7.1.B3Bo 2015

[E]—dc23

2014031479

Roaring Brook Press books may be purchased for business or promotional use.
For information on bulk purchases please contact Macmillan Corporate and Premium Sales Department
at (800) 221-7945 x5442 or by email at specialmarkets@macmillan.com.

First edition 2015
Book design by Jennifer Browne
Printed in China by Toppan Leefung Printing Ltd.,
Dongguan City, Guangdong Province

1 3 5 7 9 10 8 6 4 2

For my mom, who has always been there for me;
Aaron, who will always be there for me;
and to Vincent and my dad, who will always be with me.

BUCKLEY and his mama lived in a small wooden house by the sea.
They didn't have much, but they always had each other.

Buckley loved the beach and the things he found there.

And he loved to make things
with his hands.

Making boats out of driftwood was his favorite thing of all.

"Mama, look what I made for Papa!" said Buckley.

"What a wonderful boat! Your
papa would be proud!"
said Mama.

"I wish I could show it to him," said Buckley. He missed his papa.

A few days later it was Buckley's birthday. He and Mama
had a glorious time. She gave him a brand new set of
paints and brushes for making his boats.

That evening, Buckley and Mama went for a walk. Buckley brought along the little boat he had made especially for Papa with a note attached that said, "For Papa. Love, Buckley."

"I'm going to send my boat to Papa. If it doesn't come back to shore, I'll know he got it!" said Buckley as he placed his little boat in the water. They watched it bob up and down as the tide carried it gently out to sea.

"Mama, can I send more boats to Papa?"

"Of course you can," said
Mama. "I think he would
really like that."

After Buckley had drifted off to sleep,
Mama went out onto the beach and thought
about Papa. She missed him too.

After that, on special days Mama and Buckley
would take long walks on the beach so that he
could send one of his boats off into the ocean.

And on each one, Buckley tied a note that read:

For Papa
Love, Buckley

Buckley worked hard to make new boats all the time.

Big boats,

small boats,

long boats,

short boats,

boats with real sails, ropes, and even tiny anchors.

And each time he made a new boat,
it was even better than the last.

Buckley sent his favorite boats to Papa.
He always took extra special care to make
those the most beautiful of all.

Soon it was Buckley's next birthday.
They built a fort, played pirates, and looked
for buried treasure on the beach. Mama even made
Buckley a very special cake in the shape of a boat!

At sunset, they went for their walk to
send a boat to Papa. Suddenly Buckley
realized he'd forgotten to write a message.

"I'll be right back. I need to go write my note, so
Papa knows the boat is for him," he said anxiously.

He went into Mama's room to get some paper from her desk. As he lifted up the lid, he found all the wooden boats he had sent to Papa.

"My boats! What's Mama doing with my boats?"

Buckley closed
the lid and sat quietly.
The boats must have washed
back onto the beach, after all.
They had never reached Papa.

Mama was waiting for him on the beach. Buckley slipped
his note into the hull of the boat and placed it in the water.
Together, they watched it drift off to sea.

After their long day, Mama
tucked Buckley into bed.

"Thank you, Mama. I had a really great
birthday," he said with a yawn.
"And thank you for making every
day so wonderful too."

"You're welcome, sweetheart. I love you,"
said Mama, and she kissed him goodnight.

Mama walked to the beach. She looked out to sea and
thought about Papa. Carefully, she pulled Buckley's
boat from the kelp and brushed off the sand. As she
wrapped it gently in her shawl, she saw the note
Buckley had written. It read: